For Mama, who knows how to make it a party
—A.M.R.

For Andersson
     —C.S.

ISBN 978-1-338-65450-9

Text copyright © 2019 by Anica Mrose Rissi. Illustrations copyright © 2019 by Charles Santoso. All rights reserved. Published by Scholastic Inc., 557 Broadway, New York, NY 10012, by arrangement with Hyperion Books for Children, an imprint of Disney Book Group. SCHOLASTIC and associated logos are trademarks and/or registered trademarks of Scholastic Inc.

The publisher does not have any control over and does not assume any responsibility for author or third-party websites or their content.

12 11 10 9 8 7 6 5 4 3 2 1   20 21 22 23 24 25

                                       40

Printed in the U.S.A.

First Scholastic printing, January 2020

This book is set in Rockwell Std/Monotype.
Designed by Charles Santoso and Tyler Nevins

WATCH OUT FOR WOLF!

Written by
Anica Mrose Rissi

Illustrated by
Charles Santoso

SCHOLASTIC INC.

This little piggy went to market
for some flour and sugar, some butter and eggs,
and some chocolate for the cake.

"Watch out for Wolf,"
the other piggies warned.

"I'll be careful," Piggle swore.

"And don't forget the milk!"

This little piggy stayed home through the morning
to blow up balloons, twist streamers, wrap prizes,
and try out noisemakers and hats.

"There's Wolf!" Piggums cried. "Close the shutters! Quick!"

"Is she gone?"
Piggleton asked.

Piggums peeked. "I think so."

The piggies agreed:
"That was close."

The third little piggy
sped over the river

and through the woods,

from hutch to hole to burrow to nest,

with her basket full of invitations.

"Beware," Owl said.
"Wolf just passed this way."

"Eeek!" Piggit squealed.
"She might see me!"

"That could be disastrous,"
Frog croaked.

Piggit hurried home and changed into her best dress, while
Pigbert helped Piggle frost and decorate the cake.

Piggums picked a posy to finish the bouquet,
and Piggleton tried the roast beets.

Everything was ready.
Everything except . . .

"Welcome, welcome!" Piggums said.
"Welcome to the party. Hurry, come inside!"

This little piggy was the lookout.
She sounded the alarm.
"The wolf is coming, the wolf is coming!"

The smallest little piggy squeaked,
"Wee wee wee! Everybody hide!"

The animals leaped to their hiding places,
right in the nick of time.

Wolf banged
on the door.

"Little pigs,
little pigs,"
she called.

The piggies huddled closer.
They dared not make a sound.

The door creaked open.

The animals jumped
and screamed.

RISE!

"Happy birthday, Wolf!"

"We baked you a cake," Piggle said. "Make a wish!"

The little piggies gathered round
as Wolf's jaws opened wide.

She huffed and she puffed and
she blew the candles out

in one ferocious breath.

Anica Mrose Rissi grew up on an island off the coast of Maine, where she read a lot of books and loved a lot of pets. She now tells and collects stories, makes up songs on her violin, and eats lots of cheese with her friends in Princeton, New Jersey, where she lives with her dog, Arugula. She is also the author of *The Teacher's Pet*, illustrated by Zachariah OHora, and the Anna, Banana chapter-book series.

Charles Santoso loves drawing little things in his little journal and dreams about funny, wondrous stories. Some books he's illustrated include *I Don't Like Koala* by Sean Ferrell, *Ida, Always* by Caron Levis, *Penguin & Tiny Shrimp Don't Do Bedtime* by Cate Berry, and the *New York Times* best seller *Wishtree* by Katherine Applegate. He is currently working in sunny Singapore.